To my only love

獻給我唯一的愛

目錄

目錄

目錄

Yau Noi: The Master of Abstraction's Word Architecture

Cheng Yishen

When I read Yau Noi's poems, I came to understand that Chinese characters are a kind of micro-architecture. Yau Noi's poems use hanzi to construct exquisite buildings, which take their shape from the power of his mind at different moments. In other words, these buildings are like the supple flesh surrounding a free and independent heart. On the surface, his poems are full of pillars and flying eaves, but they are all counterparts to the soul. The heart is the source of his poetry, which means that his poems are essentially abstract. Looking carefully at his precise and vivid word architecture, Yau Noi can be said to be the most outstanding contemporary abstract poet.

Two hundred years ago, the philosopher Hegel foresaw the abstract direction in art: painting since Cubism, absolute music and stream of consciousness literature all attest to this. It should be said that Yau Noi is an expert in this tendency. A landscape emerges out of his lines. The complexity lies in the condensation, depth, and comprehensiveness of his poetry. Its condensation is the result of a long-distance, bird's eye view of the mortal world. Its depth is demonstrated by a grasp of the inevitable consequences of things in relation to their context. Its comprehensiveness is the expansion of the author's emotion and thoughts. In short, everything follows the heart, the heart spurs things forward, allowing Yau Noi's poetry to achieve a heterogenous effect, full of limitless tension and exquisite balance. Compression, depth, and synthesis are what give Yau Noi's poetry its pervasive sense of mystery. Mystery is the kernel of abstract poetry; it is a concentrated display of poetic genius. It transcends the blind imitation of realism, making the work a new construction in the truest sense: its images are familiar, but the composition of its imagery is exceptionally novel.

Yau Noi's poems demonstrate exceptional skill, without a trace of artifice. He writes under a veil of secrecy and refuses to join any poetic associations. His confidence comes from his poetic building techniques which are subordinate to the deep feeling they convey: a mode of creation dedicated to constructing beautiful images that reveal his true heart. Yau Noi continues the magnificent Chinese tradition of advancing outstanding new forms in changing circumstances, thus presenting new opportunities for the ancient Chinese poem in the literary global village. It is widely known that the creator of the Classical Chinese poem always had a certain dignity, embodied by the rigid order "Let the lord be a lord, the vassal a vassal, the father a father, and the son a son." These poems by Yau Noi display modern notions of independence and equity, and the resulting critical orientation and expression of love. Without the individual's independence and equality, Yau Noi would not be able to express such a comprehensive critique and it would be impossible to write about real love. This is to say, Yau Noi's abstract lyrics are pure modern Chinese poetry.

The author holds a doctorate in literature from Peking University.

右奈：從不炫技的抽象派大師

　　讀了右奈的詩歌，我才領悟到漢字其實是一種微型建築，右奈的漢語詩歌就是用漢字組成的精緻建築，賦予其形狀的基本力量是他不同時刻的心靈。換句話說，這些建築如同柔韌的肉體簇擁著他那顆追求獨立自由之心。表面上看，右奈的詩充滿了廊柱飛檐，其實這些都是心靈的對應物。心，乃詩之源，這就決定了他的詩實質上是抽象的，細品這些中正靈動的詞語建築，右奈可謂當代最傑出的抽象派詩人。

　　早在兩百年前，哲學家黑格爾就預見了藝術的抽象化趨勢，立體派以來的抽象繪畫，無標題音樂，意識流小說，如此等等，皆為確證。在詩歌中便是抽象的抒情，詩意的沉思。應該說，右奈深諳這種動向，他筆下的詞語呈現出一種線條式景觀，但這是一種複雜的線條，其複雜體現在它的壓縮性、立體性與綜合性。壓縮性是在遠距離觀照中對塵世萬物進行的鳥瞰式整合，立體性則是把物置於相關物的背景中加以把握的必然結果，綜合性則是由於物滲透了主體情思而導致的極度膨脹。總之，物跟隨心，心驅動物，這就使右奈的詩在心物之間達成了異質混成的效果，充滿了無限張力與精妙平衡。壓縮、立體與綜合也促成了右奈詩歌中無所不在的神秘氣息，事實上，這種神秘正是抽象詩歌的內核，是詩人創造力的集中顯示。它極大地超越了寫實藝術的亦步亦趨，使作品成為真正意義上的全新重構：其中的意象是熟悉的，而意象的組織卻是異常新奇的。

　　右奈的詩富於技藝，但並無炫技的痕跡。他以大隱的狀態思考寫作。拒絕加入任何詩人圈子。他的自信來源於他的詩歌築造技藝，完全服從於表達深邃情感的需要，是一種致力於塑造美麗形象以突顯其本心的造物。右奈顯然繼承了中國詩歌情景交融的優秀傳統，在文學地球村的新情勢下進行了傑出的變構，從而使古老的漢語詩歌呈現出某種生機。眾所周知，中國古典詩歌的創造者總體上有一種依附人格，體現了君君臣臣父父子子的頑固秩序，而右奈的這些詩充分彰顯了獨立平等的現代觀念，以及由此生發的批判傾向與愛欲表達。右奈的這些短詩表明，沒有個體的獨立人格與平等觀念，根本不可能展開徹底的批判，也不可能獲得，當然也不可能寫出，真正的愛情。就此而言，右奈的這些抽象的抒情堪稱純正的現代漢語詩歌。

作者：程一身，北京大學文學博士

014

Three Poems
三首詩
2003

Bloom

after your face changes shapes, red becomes white
blooms in the depths of your throat, a windstorm with no escape

blooms circle inside your chest,
burnishing your body and the void

fissures of pink, purple and brown remain
flickering posture straightens with age

花

你的臉變形後，紅色變成白色
花在喉嚨深處，沒有出路的風暴

花回旋在胸腔內
擦亮你全身並空曠

花留下粉色紫色褐色裂縫
搖曳的姿勢從中年挺到晚年

Borrow

borrowed day. borrowed earth collapses and curls
the death before death borrowed life
radiance nestled in the embrace of darkness

she emerges in front of your eyes
Autumn Equinox. spirits dancing at full moon
a borrowed book in its conspicuous corner
when you asked of the beginning, I remembered the mystery of birth[1]

1.Genesis 1: In the beginning God created the heavens and the earth. Now the earth was formless and empty, darkness was over the surface of the deep, and the Spirit of God was hovering over the waters. And God said, "Let there be light," and there was light. God saw that the light was good, and he separated the light from the darkness. God called the light "day," and the darkness he called "night." And there was evening, and there was morning—the first day.

借

借天。借居的大地倒塌又捲起
死亡前的死亡。借來生活
光明坐在黑暗的懷裡

她出現在你面前
秋分。幽靈在月圓時起舞
借來的書放在顯眼處
你問<u>起初</u>[1]時，我想起出生的奧秘

1.《聖經·創世紀》第一章: 起初, 神創造天地。地是空虛混沌, 淵面黑暗; 神的靈運行在水面上。
神說: 「要有光。」就有了光。神看光是好的, 就把光暗分開了。神稱光為晝, 稱暗為夜。
有晚上, 有早晨, 這是頭一日。

Flute

I am your flute, the wild animal clasped between your fingertips
a mountain range that occasions these parts, roaming the land behind us

I am your flute, replete with holes with ribs
after autumn's surgery, stuck in the same place

air carries your warmth. wake the music in recesses of flesh
listen. exhaust the beauty of the day until its spine shatters

笛 子

我是你的笛子，我是你手指間的獸
一座偶爾來此的山脈，在我們身後漫遊

我是你的笛子，有孔有肋骨
秋天做完手術，坐在原地

氣流帶著你的體溫。喚醒肉體深處的音樂
聆聽。耗盡良辰直到脊椎分裂

Five Serenades
小夜曲 五首
2005

Words

papermaking multiplies words. the textbook
altered many times. memories felled the black forest

his face ablaze

birds go back and forth to the branches of millennia past
he is crucified in a concentration camp

字

造紙術讓字繁衍。課本
被多次篡改。記憶伐光黑森林

他臉上有光

鳥往返於千年前樹枝
他被釘在集中營

Serenade

you've gone to sleep on the precipice. swans awake
and take to the serene night sky. we are not animals
why linger in wilderness?

city walls swell in the leaden night. laborers shut away awaiting orders
light returns to yesteryear. midnight's song erupts
pawns guard the palace

I am alive. waiting for you to grow up

小夜曲

你在懸崖上睡去，天鵝醒來就飛往
寧靜的星空。我們不是野獸
為何在曠野上徘徊

夜色下城牆膨脹。圈住待命的雜役
光返回往昔。午夜歌聲驟起
走卒們護衛著皇宮

我活著。等你長大

Mountain Peak

funeral goers careen in place. rising like
a eunuch returning to his homeland. grey geese cross the ravine

our era is a dull pain. fifty-seven anti-inflammatories
a toothache that torments our nerves

how many ruined by despotic rule
vapor of time, ascending in a moment of mercy

red wind blasts a thousand paper cranes ragged
never to take wing again, muddying autumn's alley

孤 山

送葬者在原地掉頭。抬著同類
宦官回歸故土。雁過山空

我的時代單調。五十七種消炎藥
牙痛折磨著下頜神經

暴政斷送了多少抗爭者
時光蒸發，升騰出片刻慈悲

紅風吹破千紙鶴
無法飄起，卻沾滿秋天的小徑

Lotus

lotus is my lover, pure and carefree
she sits on the hillside, lost in thought
eyes full of spring.

she sprouts like a rose. eagles circle overhead.
divinity's subterranean scent
suddenly ascends.

蓮花

我的愛人是純淨悠閑的蓮花，
她坐在山坡上發呆時，
眼裡有春天的景象。

她發芽如薔薇。海雕在她頭頂盤旋。
我嗅出神的氣息，
從地下突然上升到這個世界。

Rhetorical Question

our deaths are not the same
you die quietly in your sleep, while I go clear-headed and sober

I have never met you, but I stitch you into my body
and take you to see the scenes. I collapse the high wall

for a dignified death
and collect your jet-black hair

反 問

我和你死得不一樣
你在睡眠中死去，我在清醒中死去

我從未見過你，卻把你縫在身上
帶著你遊遍山川。我推倒增高的牆

為了死得體面
我珍藏著你烏黑的頭髮

Eight Music Instruments
八種樂器
2001

Piano

leaving its teeth marks on Taipei's emerald green
nipple. humanity's cradle

tides of lust raise their plumed hammer
progenitors. contaminated posterity

sound of the zither raises the stamen of time, tall and straight
the bachelor, falls back in place

鋼 琴

在臺北翠綠上留下齒痕
乳尖。人類的搖籃

情慾的潮汐，撩起帶羽毛的錘子
前輩。污染過後代

琴聲豎起光陰的花柱，挺拔的
鰈夫，跌回原地

Marimba

hurricane and drizzle; violet and delirium
emerge from the marimba. stones gather lingering clouds

lakeside, a white crane overhead
alpacas' quiet copulation. plants thick stems

a peasant woman steps on love's summit
after the deceit, squatting in the sunflowers of salty shoals

馬林巴琴

暴風與細雨；紫色與夢囈
來自馬林巴琴。石頭聚成纏綿的雲

湖畔，白鶴飛過
駝羊安靜交配。植物莖部長粗

農婦踏上愛情峰頂
上當後，蹲在鹽鹼灘的葵花裡

Cello

reverberation and joy. sweetness and sex
before the human realm like fairyland

thirteen white cranes stalk in shallow water
before the glacial drift

before the ancestral cottages and boats
lay submerged in the sea

before I arrived at the other shore with the cranes
and witnessed the purgatory

大提琴

高亢與喜悅。甜蜜與性
那時，人間恍如仙境

十三只白鷺在淺水裡行走
那時，冰川尚未漂移

那時，祖先的茅屋與木船
尚未沉於海底

那時，我跟著白頭鷹到達彼岸
尚未目睹煉獄

Double Bass

bass. bass. base...
the magnanimous skull will not lower itself...

enmity swirls...
terror tests the limits of humanity...
scrape out the sores. scrape out slander...

those closest to you not yet swallowed up...
who will be your neighbor?
life less than one...

smaller than a single tear...

低音提琴

低音。低。更低……
高貴的頭顱，絕不低下……

仇恨旋轉時……
恐怖探測人性的邊際……
剜去毒瘡。剜去惡……

離你最近而未被吞噬的……
鄰居，由何人構成……
性命有時小於一……

小於一滴淚……

Concert Flute

when you stripped off daylight's shell. dewdrops of hard drinking
clarity of the flute. spirit turned silver

when you simmered the pitch-black ending
the bitter longing of dawn. stood alone

when you returned freedom to the good
ocean and air remained; gullies and sunshine

when you straightened the vertebrae in your spine
no need to choose between good and wrong. you are your own path

when you stand for a long time on the horizon
blackness cuts across humanity's shadow

長 笛

當你剝掉白天的殼。狂飲愛的露珠
長笛的清亮。讓心靈變成銀色

當你熬過漆黑的結尾
苦盼破曉時分。孤身而立

當你把自由還給善良的人
還剩下空氣海洋；山谷與陽光

當你挺起脊椎動物的脊梁
無需選擇對與錯。你是你的道

當你佇立地平線上
人類的背影有一刻真黑

Trumpet

droplets of the virus infect the land
my companion returns to her old abode. the locked-down city stifling...

illusion opens its own ballet and symphony
air furtive and tender, life ensnared in a net

bar-headed goose on its interstellar passage. young buds whisper
vaccinated traveler. shouldering his bag
the riverbed runs dry, rotting into mud

小 號

病毒以飛沫傳染山河
伴侶退回舊舍。幾乎窒息的封城……

幻覺張開芭蕾與交響樂
空氣詭秘而清甜，生命困於網中

斑頭雁往返星際。幼芽竊竊私語
旅行者打完疫苗。背起行囊
斷流的河床，腐爛之物化為泥土

Gong

preacher struggles to contain his grin, king completed the Via Crucis
woman takes off her veil, wipes up his blood stain

the hustle and bustle of gong. as if mallet hitting human head
truly I say to you, today you will be with me in Paradise[2]

betray the master for the sake of glory. old business
let you play with fire and get burned. let you be crazy for half a year

give me water[3]

2. Luke 23:43
3. John 19:28

芒鑼

布道者愁容滿面，王走完苦路
婦人摘下憂傷面紗，擦拭他的血跡

鑼聲喧囂。像木槌撞上人頭
我實在告訴你，今日你要同我在樂園了[2]

賣主求榮。古老的生意
讓你玩火自焚。讓你多瘋半年

我渴了[3]

2. 路加福音 23:43
3. 約翰福音 19:28

Drum

multiplicity of bison, running wild to the azure
mongolians beat their drums on the plateau

white horse shaves the forehead clean
in the dazzling yellow river

spawn of seven fish
pregnant with culture

鼓

綿延的野牛，奔向蒼穹
黃種人擂起高原的鼓

白馬剃亮額頭
在金燦燦的大河裡

七條大魚產下的卵
孕育了文明

Eleven Poems for Michelle
給 Michelle 十一首
2004

Fan

love detects the color of your heart
Michelle in the mirror, it's sunday
summer suddenly shows its hand. you've lost your fan
rebirth after the roses' withering
in my nights of absence, what troubles have you encountered

we thanked the surgeon, he seemed like a veterinarian
your pure eyes in the opera house, glistening in the night
remind me of the lotus' haughtiness on the hilltop
tossing out the expired salt you embrace me, ice and mink hide melt away
in my love for you, unable to see the true shape of the universe

扇 子

愛檢測出你心臟的顏色
Michelle 在鏡子裡，現在是星期天
夏天亮出它的底牌。你丟下扇子
玫瑰凋零後再次復活
在我缺席的夜晚，你遇到什麼難題

我們感謝外科醫生，他看上去像獸醫
你純潔的眼睛，在歌劇院在午夜閃亮
讓我想起山頂上傲慢的雪蓮
你扔掉過期的鹽就和我接吻，冰和貂皮不見了
我愛你，卻看不清宇宙的形狀

Mirror

mountain range meanders in ink wash. lips of love
wetted. secret river cuts through
bowels of the jungle. beauty waiting

musical instruments. god's fingerprints
I hand you your comb. funereal flowers
a classical conception. and me, ugly and past my prime

鏡 子

山巒漫遊在水墨畫裡。愛之唇
濕潤。一條秘密的河隱匿
密林深處。美在等待

樂器。上帝的指紋
我遞給你梳子。葬花
古典意境。我因衰老而醜陋

Comb

I love you

hair long or short
I've borrowed your light. you are a light
emperor concealed under the arch of your foot, plants grow in your direction
I hold you. plum blossoms flower, the river swells and perch grow fat[4]

concubine shrinks back. gathering seeds
let me rest peacefully next to you. reclining on your side
you ask about a little shop on nanlouguxiang. the thick-toothed comb
I remember the carpenter's love[5]. a set of jade

---

4. "In front of western hills white egrets fly up and down. Over peach-mirrored stream, where perches are full grown." A Fisherman's Song by Zhang Zhihe, a Tang dynasty poet.
5. Poet Gu Cheng worked as a carpenter.

梳 子

愛你

無論你留長髮還是短髮
我借過你的燈光！你是燈光
天子伏在你腳下，有根之物向你聚攏
我抱起你。桃花流水鱖魚肥[4]

小妾收縮。捕獲種子
讓我安睡在你身邊。俯臥再側臥
問起南鑼鼓巷小店。粗齒梳
想起木匠的愛情[5]。珏

4. 出自唐代詩人張志和的《漁歌子》：西塞山前白鷺飛, 桃花流水鱖魚肥。
5. 詩人顧城做過木匠。

Nanlouguxiang[6]

the comb vendor, a note of thanksgiving
he barters with the swiftness of an avalanche
lanterns hung at the market entranceway

hailstones smash down on the yellow front-loader
impassioned animal gnashing its teeth in the depth of night. teeth crumbing with decay
reverberate as if shouted off a mountaintop

you drape yourself in your nightgown and go to the kitchen
I am just behind you. white cat mews thrice
you cover your face with your nightgown

6. Nanluoguxiang is a narrow alley in the Beijing city.

南鑼鼓巷[6]

賣梳子的小販，像感恩節的註解
打折時，臉上有雪崩的節奏
燈籠掛在超市入口

冰雹砸落外環的黃色鏟車
罪獸在深夜磨牙。那些蛀牙隨時斷裂
山斷裂的聲音此起彼伏

你披上睡衣走向廚房
我跟在你身後。白猫叫了三聲
拽著睡衣蓋住臉

6. 南鑼鼓巷是北京的一條胡同。

White Cat

when you're angry, you may encounter the most despicable character
at the summit, a black cat leaps to the moon
abandoning mercy. as water flows on

leading to the newlyweds' nest on high, the bridegroom scales its walls
your face source of the depth of sorrow. the cat looks to Chang'e
wildflowers burst open in vain. as water flows on

白 貓

生氣時，你會看到討厭的人
在高峰，黑貓跳上月亮
捨棄憐憫。<u>水在流</u>

通往新婚的懸崖，新郎沿著絕壁攀登
你的臉令人心碎，黑貓望向嫦娥
野花猛然開遍空虛。水在流

As Water Flows On

in the sultry dawn, bar-headed geese encircle the mountain range
collapsing wind and image. the expanse of mountains
a sick person dressed in sanctity's trousers

seclusion of thought pushes you backward
a dull thunder haunts apprehensive animals
the nurse's riddle strikes your forehead dark. before it all collapses

水在流

悶熱的清晨，棕頭雁盤旋在山脈之上
倒塌的風和偶像。山在長
病人穿上尊嚴的褲子

隱居的念頭逼著我往回走
悶雷侵擾疑惑的動物
護士的謎語讓額頭變暗。在坍塌之前

Riddle

I can see you're insane, far off from reality today
thinking of your lover, the mountain lights
don't entrust grief to the dead
you are at once cramped and isolated by the world

who are you? you survey the scene from a remote location
looking out at what you have looked out at, again
propping up your uncollapsing face. a human face
you are a seraph. cradling your arms, you stand alone in the world

謎 語

我看見你瘋了，今天出走人間
想起愛人，山外的燈
不要在逝者身上寄托憂傷
你逼仄卻被眾人孤立

你是誰？在山峰側身眺望
把看過的又看一遍
撐持你不倒的是臉。人臉
你是女神。抱著雙臂獨立於世

Face

your face concealed another face
blockage in a taxi driver's facial veins
a lover's face emerges before your eyes

I am your exterior. I want to stroke your dark hair
icy torrent down your back dissipates at your tailbone
abandoning this city of death

the spirit of death has his eyes set on you
another shadow engulfs your own
I want you. even after the twists and turns

臉

你的臉上隱藏著另一張臉
出租車司機臉上靜脈堵塞了
情人在臉上浮現

我在你外面。我想摸你黑頭髮
寒流順著背部從尾骨消散
拋棄這座僵死的城市

死神緊緊盯著你
你的陰影裡有別人的陰影
我要你。波折之後

Cold Wave

love is a starving night beast
lust. splashing in red wine
a bird outside the window stepping on another bird

teach me to repair the world. heaven above heaven
ancient apes in their elevation. observe into the distance
I've lost my lofty aim
in my slow sinking, before I disappear

I push you to a higher place

寒 流

愛情像一只飢渴的夜獸
慾望。濺落在紅酒裡
鳥在窗外踩著另一隻鳥
請教我補天，天外天
<u>高處的古猿</u>，瞭望遠方
我失去崇高目的
緩慢下降，在沉沒之前

把你推到高處

Ancient Apes in their Elevation

it's over
in the classroom, children come across a math problem
when you left antiquity
dinosaurs were still dreaming in the night. I want to see you again

life rocks us arrhythmic
I drop below. expelled
a stream of frozen trains in the north

Myself and my fate are the same
winding bandages. to leave bruises
old wounds rubbed raw

高處的古猿

結束了
課堂上，孩子們碰到數學難題
你在遠古時離開了
恐龍做夢的夜晚。我想再次碰見你

生活讓人震驚卻沒有節奏
我掉在下面。被驅逐
北方鐵軌上停著一列結冰的火車

我和我的命運一樣
纏著繃帶。留下悔恨
舊傷摩擦新傷

It's Over

don't shed tears for me. only death can stop me
you are your shell
your future
sprouts

unrestful age. your heart is also ill at ease
I am not sentimental or afraid
landscapes drift away
fire freezing over

outside of myself. you see my shadow
and hear my voice
but it's not me

please take away the fan

結束了

別為我哭泣。唯有死神讓我停下
你是你的外殼
未來是你的
你發芽

不安的年齡。你有不安的心
我不傷感也不害怕
江山漂走了
火結冰了

我在我之外。你看到我的身影
聽到我的聲音
那不是我

請拿走扇子

Eleven Kitchen Arias
廚房詠嘆調 十一首
2017

Salt

there was salt in that bright kitchen. first love was our dreary supper
you are a nymph, just as salt is a nymph. rosefinch knows nothing of the rose
Michelle, where did you leave your fan?

a piano sounds in the depth of the night. your joy is salty
we detain life's breath with fine wine
outside the kitchen. mume blossoms unfold

<u>鹽</u>

那雪亮的廚房有鹽。初戀是我們單調的晚餐
你是仙女。鹽也是仙女。朱雀不懂玫瑰
Michelle 你的扇子丟在哪兒呢

鋼琴在深夜。你的歡樂是鹹的
我們用美酒挽留人生
廚房外。紅梅開

Braised Carp

roving in the flame. she is crazed
my fingertip fixed on a single word: ripple
fish head cooked through, tail flapping foolishly

everything forgotten. including happiness
the tortured flesh annihilated
not burnished, but melded

紅燜鯉魚

她在火焰裡遊動。頓時瘋了
我想摁住一個詞：漣漪
魚頭熟了，魚尾還在喜劇般擺動

忘記一切。包括忘記幸福
酷刑消滅肉體
它沒有被燒紅而是被燜紅

Long-handled Spoon

wafting aroma of venison, ladled into porcelain
a winter stew. wine-colored hue deepens
pass me a long-handled spoon.

my eyes settle on you. in the kitchen preparing the spices
outside, the heavy snow wills the branches to break
a deer walks into my field of vision, as if of my own volition

he gazes at me. turns in an instant and disappears
your cheeks reflecting red in the flames. removing your sweater
scatter the pollen of love

長柄勺

這些味道鮮美的鹿肉，盛在青花瓷碗裡
熟於冬季。顏色由鮮紅變深
請遞給我長柄湯勺

我凝視著你。在廚房準備調料
窗外，大雪任意壓斷樹枝
一只鹿凝視著我，我猜測它來此的意圖

它望著我。隨即轉身隱去
火焰映紅臉頰。你脫掉厚毛衣
撒下愛情花粉

Radish and Carrot

la marseillaise drifts into the kitchen. Hong Kong
radish and carrot nestled against the crude cutting block
clean | firm | feverish | enduring
when it flows, water is love's dictionary

Michelle reads leisurely, like a verb in hiding
warming itself in a bird's lair
following the lilies, hand extended upward
the maid's legs unswerving as she washes

白蘿蔔與胡蘿蔔

馬賽曲飄進廚房，香港
兩只蘿蔔依偎在粗糙的刀俎上
幹淨 | 堅挺 | 發熱 | 持久
它流動時，水是愛的詞典

Michelle 悠閑地看書，像動詞隱蔽著
被雀鳥佔據的巢穴漸暖
順著百合花，手從底部往上
女傭洗淨它的時候，併攏了雙腿

Scallion and Ginger

goose intestines dipped in hotpot. see you tomorrow at chater garden
god of cookery hears the coronet. this is the future
arriving early

beasts of memory boil oval eggs
fifteen. spitting blood in the breeze

take care of yourself. forced southeast
wild birds circle the temple
embrace the night, plucking flowers

蔥和生薑

火鍋涮鵝腸。明天遮打花園見
食神聽見號角。這就是未來
提前來了

記憶之獸滾落一堆橢圓的蛋
十五歲。微風中吐過鮮血

看守自己。偏安東南
野鳥繞著神廟轉圈
抱香夜，插小花

Greedy Eater[7]

stew the beef simmer the lamb pig head pig ear
pig tongue pig tail stewed with soybeans
nanjing duck soup yangzhou goose guiyang chicken soup

steamed salted ribbonfish fresh butterfish
a whole perch carp and beancurd soup
steamed mackerel tormented

egg-filled dumplings meat-filled dumplings salted egg egg-fried rice
meatballs bacon braised pork bones left for the dog
cured meat cured meat cured meat cured meat

yesterday. cured meat lodged between the teeth
gums languishing in their softness. lap up the daisy and the lotus
dark mouth engulfs strong liquor. your ardent death

lard! lard! lard! lard!
pig head. pig head. pig head.

7. Greedy eater, a suzhou dialect, a proper noun for the elders to scold at gluttonous children.

觸 祭[7]

燉牛肉 煨羊肉 豬耳朵
豬舌頭 豬尾巴燉黃豆
南京老鴨湯 揚州老鵝 貴陽雞湯

蒸鹹帶魚 鮮鯧魚
整條鱖魚 鯽魚豆腐湯
白蒸青魚 煎熬

蛋餃 鹹蛋 蛋炒飯
肉圓 鹹肉 紅燒肉 骨頭餵夠狗
臘肉 臘肉 臘肉 臘肉

昨天。臘肉塞住崩壞的牙縫
口腔糜爛。舔雛菊舔蓮花
黑暗吞噬烈酒。你烈 你必死

豬油! 豬油! 豬油! 豬油!
豬頭。豬頭。豬頭。

7. 觸祭，蘇州方言，長輩罵小孩子貪吃的專用詞。

Kung Pao Chicken

dry firewood and blazing fire, braised chicken
seven glasses of moutai, stir-fry Guizhou dried chillies

the palace guardian takes pleasure in what the eunuch lacks[8]
the empress dowager allows him more than he is entitled

8. The palace guardian of Qing Dynasty is called "Gongbao". Ding Baozhen, the head of Shandong, was a native of Guizhou, with strong temperament and love for spicy food. He used the practice of stir-frying dried chillies and braising chicken in Sichuan cuisine, which made the home-style dish "Kung Pao Chicken" widely popular. In the eighth year of Tongzhi in the Qing Dynasty, Ding Baozhen executed the great eunuch An Dehai for his crimes and made him take off his pants to make a fool of himself.

宮保雞丁

幹柴烈火。燜雞丁
七杯茅臺。爆炒貴州幹辣椒

宮保陰莖堅挺。太監沒有陽具[8]
太后樂，一根乩耙往裡戳

8. 清朝對總督的尊稱叫「宮保」。時任山東總督丁寶楨是貴州人，性情剛烈愛吃辣。
他以川菜中先爆炒幹辣椒再加上燜雞丁的做法，使「宮保雞丁」這道家常菜廣為流傳。
丁寶楨在清朝同治八年按罪處決了大太監安德海，並讓他當眾脫下褲子出醜。

Peking Duck

we praise: spooky palate
flaming oven, comes like the fleshly truth

sweet dream filled with feather, you were a man of tremendous promise
work indefatigably day and night, seek countermeasure for motherland

Beijing, red burning iron bars and cauldron
Beijing, redundant, corrupt, fragrant

Qing Dynasty. imperial garden kindle the fruit trees
chef who clean the stove ashes out, see the fallen cervical vertebrae

北京烤鴨

我們讚美：幽靈般的味覺
火紅的烤爐，有肉香真理般襲來

美夢填滿羽毛，你本是棟梁之材
日夜操勞，尋求國與家的對策

北京，燒紅的鐵條和大鼎
北京，沈重的，腐敗的，芬芳的

大清。皇家園林燃起果木
清除爐灰的大廚，看見掉下的頸椎

Chives

winter solstice of the gengzi year. winter colder than before
stock prices leap cross the seven peaks
the chives deep green, extending in all directions
raise the sickle, mow down

I went out to buy tofu, Snakeheaded fish and oysters for soup
distant mountains curl like eyebrows   deeply savory
you will rise above the others
mowed down

韭菜

庚子年冬至。比以往冷寒
股價躍過七座山峰
韭菜碧綠，一望無際
手起刀落，割

我出門買豆腐黑魚牡蠣做湯
遠山如黛　鮮味正濃
你將脫穎而出
割

Occasionally When Steaming Sea Bream

lovers of beautiful scenery need not go to Edinburgh
fishermen let go the boat on sky
flowers in the small courtyard bloom of their own accord
rereading history books in seclusion

清蒸鯿魚時偶得

樂景何愛丁
漁夫放天舟
小庭花自詠
嫻熟弄春秋

Shallow Fry

split open man's face, cut off his feet[9]

three thousand concubines, a single stalk of scallion

9. Sun Hao, the last emperor of the state of Eastern Wu during the Three Kingdoms period (264-280 AD), indulging himself in wine and women, and being cruel in his punishments. He favored punishing people by peeling their facial skin, gouging out their eyes and cutting off their legs.

油煎

劈人面，刖人足[9]
三千妃，一根蔥

---

9. 三國時期吳國末代皇帝孫皓（公元 264 年 -280 年在位）在位時沉
溺酒色，昏庸暴虐。喜歡活剝人臉，或挖人眼珠或砍人足。

Meander, 13 Poems
辵*十三首
2019

* 辵 (chuò)，走走停停的意思

Faultline

race is a musical note. bearing witness to
morality's faultlines. imperial inheritance
for the survival of the lackeys' offspring

serving the arbitrary thick-shelled heart. chosen...
more cruel when they take power
eras pursue. who conceals

缺 口

種族是一個音符。它見證
道德的缺口。皇權世襲
奴仆的後裔得以存活

臣服於蠻橫的厚腦殼。被揀選的……
奴仆成為主子後更殘忍
世代追逐。誰遮掩

Dialogue with a Blank Piece of Paper

a fingertip alters the brain's orders. ordinary man in a high position
presses mispronounced words into the cracks of a ship's hold and sinks it in the sea

a dinner party, poolside. the attendant's temples bare blood
when she encounters fire she dances into water cries to an archeologist splits open

her proud cheekbones
flattened black

和一頁白紙對話

手指違抗大腦指令。匹夫上位
把念錯的詞釘在船艙的夾縫並沉入海底

晚宴設在池邊。侍者金色太陽穴滲血
她碰到火就舞碰到水就哭碰到考古者就碎裂

驕傲的顴骨粗壯
被黑後扁了

Chair

the emperor sits over the land. overthrown overthrown by
the flatterer that now sits on the throne. the new king...
when the chair is empty, the imperial consort elopes

scholar holds on to unofficial history. clinging for three thousand years
dynastic change cannot produce compassion. king's logic is logic
illogic

the chair stands upright in the central hall
sycophants come crawling towards it. they bow and submit
then, replace

we take afternoon tea. the chair's cracks extend
no matter the weather, what my father's generation did
I will not do

椅 子

皇上坐擁江山。被推翻 推翻他的
佞臣坐上龍椅。成為新的王……
椅子空著時，皇后私奔了

書生抱殘於野史。三千年守缺
世代更迭不會帶來憐憫。王道就是道
無道

椅子兀立在大廳中央
獻媚者向它匍匐而來。膜拜順從權勢
現在，重置

我們在午後喝茶。椅子張開裂紋
不管天氣好壞，父輩做過的事
我不做

Fireworks in March Yangzhou

a chance encounter. whitened temples. shake hands. late autumn begins in the old capital
faltering. estranged. mute.
a kettle of spirits on a frozen night. dumplings and pork

a night thinking of the twenty four distant bridges, yangzhou already a blur
light on the lake, kingfisher reflected on the sloping snow
the beloved remains in the old city

hold onto the moon. keep away from the base
light brushes your age spots
a more distant black

take shelter

煙花三月下揚州……

相逢。鬢白。握手。重遊故國晚秋
遲頓。疏遠。無語。
寒夜一壺酒。餃子豬頭肉

遙想二十四橋夜，揚州已模糊
湖泊的反光，倒映出雪坡上的翠鳥
至愛留在舊城

抱月。遠離小人
光觸及老年斑
更遠的黑

庇護著

Even the Wearied Bird of Spring Flies

rain pours down
uninterrupted words tuck you to sleep. monastic study
characters fleeing with the birds. what is your surname?
there is no one called tang in ruyiting[10]
the rule of law is actually ruling you[11]

you will meet sickness. I speak with a stone
silk/ porcelain/ the great wall/ the forbidden city
blackmail/ petitions/ domestic violence/ bullying / human trafficking
terracotta warriors/ pandas/ tasty hotpot[12]
terror/ exile/ struggle/ masturbation

on the love of the lotus: no
don't, you stupid fool
fuck, something's wrong with your head[13]

lizards short tailed elephant we shouldn't learn from qin shihuang
you will pass by a small conquered country...

10. Hunan dialect: There is no one called tang in ruyiting. Ruyiting is a place name.
11. Cantonese.
12. Sichuan dialect: it means comfortable and good.
13. Shanghai dialect: "No, no. You idiot, your brain is damaged."

春倦鳥亦飛……

下雨了。
連綿的詞帶你去午睡。僧侶的書房
字跟著鳥逃逸。你姓什麼
如意亭冒得姓湯的[10]
要依法治國，其實係要依法治你[11]

疾病是偶遇。我和一塊石頭聊天
絲綢 / 瓷器 / 長城 / 故宮
詐騙 / 訪民 / 家暴 / 霸凌 / 人販子
兵馬俑 / 大熊貓 / 火鍋巴適[12]
驚恐 / 逃亡 / 掙紮 / 擼

愛蓮說：伐來三
夠，儂只港卵
赤那，依腦子壞特啦[13]

蜥蜴 短尾象 我們不學秦始皇
你繞過被攻占的小國……

10. 湖南方言：如意亭沒有姓湯的。如意亭是地名。
11. 粵語。
12. 四川方言：「巴適」是舒服、好的意思。
13. 上海方言：不行，不要。你這個笨蛋，你腦子壞掉啦。

You[14]

young girl, young eyes, not convinced, takes another position
silly goose, you're too proud, duped, foolish
zero tolerance, beaten, contemptible, didn't learn
something arising from nothing, wheezing

taken in, finding fault, slap in the face, satisfy an itch
pull it together, little darling, head, toenails
excellent, saliva, a dear face, teasing
lost hope, up in smoke, unbearable
perturbed, death, two shots

you've got the wrong person

14. This poem is written in Suzhou dialect.

俖[14]

小娘魚，天勿亮，勿臨盆，趺角翹
阿木林，阿摸卵，阿屈死，豬頭三
咽勿落，吃頭皮，賤骨頭，勿習上
揢死空，──昏圖

捐木梢，扳錯頭，吃倪光，煞渴
收骨頭，小囡囡，顆浪頭，腳節揢
呱呱叫，饞唾水，香面孔，弄松
卵嘆氣，焦冒氣，湯不牢
濟糟，斷命，二槍

俖認錯脫人哉

你

小姑娘，小眼睛，不服氣，唱反調
呆頭鵝，你還拽，被愚弄，沒腦子
零容忍，挨打頭，賤骨頭，不學好
無中生有，──呼嚕

上當了，找岔子，打耳光，過癮
收拾，小囡囡，腦袋，腳趾甲
好極了，吐沫，親臉，作弄
失望，焦味，受不了
煩躁，可惡，公蟋蟀

你認錯人了

14. 此詩原文為蘇州方言

Sorrow Sleeping in the Time

beauty split open. on prison's cutting board
sorrow, not yet dismembered. the brilliant white flesh

brilliant, brilliant, absolute white

april. earth's convulsions
inescapable adversity. peeled-back skin drains the lust for life

when her head was split open, a flock of startled birds flew out
the tyrant reclined in heaven's serenity

heaven, heaven, the hell of heaven.

悲傷睡在時光裡

美人叉開。在監獄的案板上
一抹未肢解的悲傷。雪白的肉體

雪白，雪白，絕望的白

四月，萬物痙攣
逃不出厄運。剝皮後痛不欲生

她的頭被切開時，驚恐的鳥群飛出
暴君安詳地躺在天堂

天堂，天堂，地獄般的天堂

Tongue

tongue soft as a lotus. truth speaks with rays of light
turning the devious black. do not do evil things even though they may be insignificant
reading the scripture, sparks fly from the tongue

heresy's tongue puffs up, maintaining order through violence
eras come and go. addicted to power drink blood death
practicing crass falsehoods

principles disappearing in an instant

舌

舌軟如蓮。說真話時含光芒
使奸詐時發黑。勿以惡小而為之
誦讀聖經時，火花從舌上飛逸

異端之舌鼓起，以暴治國
世代往復。嗜權嗜酒嗜血嗜殺
練就粗俗的謊言

道須臾絕跡

Weeds[15]

moon and death eternal. my tears flow to you
I give my voice to you, breathing
from this life to previous incarnations

my shadow a ghost, final wishes of the departed
floating in the night sky, sporadic, silent
you reside in me

evening wind blows the birds red
sweet birds singing. those far away
painful, arrogant, ignorant

you have intelligence and stone
as judgement day approaches, you still haven't been born
mallards cavort on a freshwater lake

---

15. 芥 (jie), the ancient name for weed. Similar to a simplified Chinese character 芥.
Mr. Lu Xun wrote in "After Sick Talk": Since the beginning of history, Chinese people have always been slaughtered, slaved, plundered, tortured, and oppressed by their own people, experienced the pain that beyond human tolerance, and every examination make people to feel like they are not living in this world.

丯¹⁵

月亮和永別。我的淚水到達你
我的聲音傳給你，是呼吸
今生到前世

我的影子是幽靈和遺願
在夜空遊蕩，零星的，無聲的
我裡面有你

紅色的晚風，把鳥吹紅
甜蜜的鳥在唱歌。那些遠去的
痛苦的、狂妄的、無知的

你有靈性和石頭
末日來臨時，你還未出生
綠頭鴨遊弋淡水湖

---

15. 丯 (jiè)，野草的古稱。和簡體漢字豐形似。
魯迅先生在《病後雜談之余》寫道：自有歷史以來，中國人是一向被同族屠
戮、奴隸、敲掠、刑辱、壓迫下來的，非人類所能忍受的楚痛，也都身受過，
每一考查，真教人覺得不像活在人間。

The Assassin Forgives Himself

the assailant jumps for joy, martyr's day
funeral in high place, winding and rutted as it is
the very smallest flower, fallen, fate's bow strings stretched tight

who was left behind? ghosts shriek at the winding way
I see all the ages
our ancestors endured. crawling in degradation

the primal boulder guards the surface site
apes howling on both sides of the yangtze
searching for firewood, cooked meat, and written characters

ribs and blood splash, birds startle
the dead rise again. what are you cutting?
the mat[16]

16. From "A New Account of the Tales of the World: Virtuous Conduct", cut apart the sitting mat
and seat separately. Set boundaries with friends who have opposing views. Break up.

兇手寬恕了自己

兇徒雀躍，國殤日
葬於高山，必經曲折坎坷
最小的花，損落，命運之弦繃斷

誰被甩出？鬼在彎道吶喊
我看見所有年代
隱忍的祖輩。以爬行的姿勢苟活

原始的巨石鎮守地表遺址
猿在長江兩岸啼嚎
祈求炭火、熟肉與字符

肋血濺，飛鳥驚
死去的復活了，你割什麼
割席[16]

16. 出自《世說新語·德行第一》把席割開分別坐。和觀點相反的朋友劃清界線。
絕交。

Crane

—for my father

ancestors are cranes. a flock of cranes
a single crane

follows the seasons. it rises and flutters
spiraling above the marshlands
he appears from going back and forth, brings me to the right

in search of habitat
he descends on the reedy shore, by the yellow sea, in the snowy night
on the isolated hamlet, the end

a demon trails on his heels, the crowd disperses
you are suddenly torn down. burned down. only bone and ash remain
now, two spring mornings
will never meet

dad, you're gone
now, night is blacker
now, my heart is lost

while there is evil in the world
there is no more need to worry

what comes next will be much better

16:30 3/13/2019

鶴

——永別了，爹

祖先是鶴。一群鶴
一只鶴

隨季風而動。起跳撲騰
在海塗上飛來飛去
他從來去中來，把我帶到右邊

為了尋找棲息地
降臨到蘆葦灘，在黃海邊，在雪夜
在孤零零的村莊，在盡頭

兇神尾隨，人群聚散
你忽然被撕下。燒毀。剩下骨灰
從此，春天的兩個上午
永不相遇

爹，你走了
從此，黑夜更黑
從此，我心永逝

盡管世間惡人出沒
不必再擔憂

後來的肯定善良多了

16:30 3/13/2019

Farewell

farewell to this moment. contact aligner and chip

farewell to weeds growing madly in the yard. greedy neighbors stretching out their legs
fleas invade your sleep. pushed to suicide
thoughts. time abandoned in the corners

a light breeze occasionally raps on the door knocker
perhaps we have lived. come. felt
the heart, only

告 別

告別此刻。光刻機與芯

告別雜草瘋長的後院。惡鄰蹬腿
跳蚤入侵睡眠。霸凌推著輕生
念頭。時間廢棄在拐彎處

微風，偶爾輕叩門環
也許，我們活過 來過 摸過
唯有，心

Lion Rock

sawtooth lion rock extends between heaven and hell
boundary between man and beast obscured. coexisting under the peak

my window faces it. starlight circles the summit
early morning and night. they leap and retreat

only remaining descendants. carrying their genetic inheritance
they conceal the night's pearl. astride the mythical beast

獅子山

獅子山橫在天堂與地獄之間
人獸界限模糊。雜居山下

我的窗子對著它。星光環繞峰頂
有早晨有晚上。有跳動有後退

僅存的後裔。攜帶種族基因
藏起夜明珠。騎上神獸

Falling, 8 Poems
墜落 八首
2015

Jaguar and Fish

jaguar's reflection flashes bright in the mirror

I go to the market to pick up some fish, returning home
in a mirage, they have already gone back to the great rivers
as neighbors grow old

clouds prowl into a jaguar formation, on occasion,
and vanish in an instant

today, you've arrived at the last stretch of life

豹和魚

彩色的豹從鏡子裡閃過

我在集市上買魚，回家時
在錯覺中，它們已重返江河
鄰居們正慢慢變老

雲朵偶然形成一群豹的圖像
瞬間又在空中解體

今天，你走到人生的盡頭

A Farewell

in the night that belonged to lovers, good and evil alternate
we lean on our faith in survival, coming from a desolate star
between her and life, the eternal summit

fall's gone mad. a dictator swallows mercury
the path leading to slavery is far
she departs. death by ruthlessness, death by delusion, death by place of birth

訣 別

那屬於情人的夜空，善惡交替
我們賴以生存的信念，來自荒涼的星球
她和山之間，隔著永恆之巔

秋天瘋了。獨裁者吞服水銀
通往奴役之路遙遠
她死了，死於酷吏，死於幻想，死於出生地

Red Kite

darkness cradled in the breast of light
wildflowers that rock the earth
the devil carries his iron cage, wandering through the city center

fishes return to the vast ocean,
birds stand on branches higher than morality
the devil with his iron cage, seizing those who do not meet his gaze

the black-hearted functionary kidnaps the minister
with only a soft pfff

11/1/2015

紅 鳶

黑暗坐在光明的懷裡
野花搖晃著大地
惡吏提著鐵籠，在鬧市區走來走去

魚返回廣闊的海洋
鳥站在比道德更高的樹枝
惡吏提著鐵籠，捉拿不順眼的人

惡吏劫持了下臣
留下噗的一聲

2015.11.1

Wine Barrel

wine barrels fill the dreamscape. even if there is no tomorrow
death is still three decades from me
red is rich and green lean, only blue eternal

peasant woman passes by a missionary's tombstone
she doesn't understand the islands crowding at all sides
first love's grown taller

the fairytale castle floats far
never losing you, never having you
the emperor's demise. the wine barrel tumbles down from its high place

酒 桶

酒桶堆滿夢境，即使沒有未來
死神離我還有三十年
紅肥綠瘦，唯獨藍色永垂

農婦經過傳教士的墓碑
她不解於四周冒出成群的島嶼
初戀的情人長高了

童話城堡飄遠了
從未失去你，從未有過你
皇上駕崩。酒桶從高處滾下

Sea

traveler walk to the cliff, sea suddenly aged
a woman sitting in the morning, playing a flute
waves lift silver syrup, forcing the horizon to retreat
gods cover their ears, standing on the desolate celestial boundary

southern sea gentle as creation
you've arrived suddenly at old age, no need to be sad that you've been
ground to a deep green juice. consciousness and compassion
the ocean arches its back, rejecting the withered and rotten skeleton

大 海

旅行者走到懸崖，大海突然年邁
女人坐在早晨，吹笛子
海浪掀起銀色之槳，逼著地平線後退
眾神掊耳，立於蒼涼的星際

南方的海水溫潤如創世紀
你突然來到老年，不必傷感於被
磨成墨綠的汁。自覺與悲憫
大海弓起脊背，抵制枯朽的屍骨

Injure

you rupture limits. I fear laogai
a future of suffering. raise the roar of waves

buddha sprinkles salt on the sea's surface
sacred scrolls curled in the seabed

sister, as you soar
don't forget the blue and pink

戕

你扯斷底線。我懼怕勞改
苦難的前程。抬高了波濤聲

諸佛向海面撒鹽
經筒卷入海底

姐姐，你扶搖直上
別忘了淡藍色與粉紅色

Today the Mountains Appear Especially Far...

the savior scattered bitterness
time isolates you. isolates fire

trial by lie
survivors dancing on bleached bones

guards and convicts face to face
rain wiping the fatherland clear off the glass

今天的山，看上去很遠……

救世主播下苦厄
時光隔絕了你。隔絕了火

以謊言審判謊言
幸存者在白骨上跳舞

獄警與囚犯對視
雨水擦去玻璃上的祖國

Calico Cat

the devil emerges in the evening with a lion's howl
we've become slaves again, annihilated by the wilderness
lord! where is your sceptre now?

calico cat croons in the silence of the night, leaping from the heights
to its yielding homeland. skeletons thunder
the wearied crowd collapses, rising again as ghosts

花 貓

魔鬼在傍晚跳出，像獅子一樣吼叫
我們再次成為奴隸，湮滅於荒野
主啊！你的權杖在哪兒呢？

花貓在月夜靜觀，從高峰躍下
松散的家園。骸骨滾動
苦難的人群倒下，變成鬼

Return, 8 Poems
返 八首
2010

Snow Lotus

vultures carry human bones and spirits fly to the sun
when you leave with the hounds, I walk to the depression

common people succumb to vice, unwilling to yield to justice
the oppressed would rather die than resist

cuckoos fly from the memorial hall, weeping blood as they return home
after you pass. the mountains wastelands of solitude

雪 蓮

禿鷲帶著人骨和靈魂飛往太陽
你和獵犬離去時，我正走到低凹處

庶民屈服於惡習，不肯向公平讓步
被壓迫的人，寧死不反抗

杜鵑飛離祠堂，泣血而鳴歸去兮
你消逝後。空山孤立荒原

Hymn

christian chorus at night, antler at the back of the head
flashing its SOS
singing hallelujah. praise be to god. give thanks

this unusual fall. short
but unforgettable. hallelujah. praise be to god
it was short. but unforgettable.

face, flashing
meteors burst at the brink
hallelujah. praise be to god

聖 歌

基督徒在夜間合唱，額頭上方的犄角
閃爍著求救信息
他們唱著**哈利路亞贊美主**。感恩

這個秋天不同尋常。它很短
卻難忘。**哈利路亞贊美主**
它很短。卻難忘。

臉，閃爍著
流星在邊緣落地開花
哈利路亞贊美主

New Orleans Summer: Crimson
Kumquat and Charcoal

wildflowers lift up mountains. sleepwalking
I fly to the sea while the land rises

woman's descendants injure your head
satan's descendants become enemies

devil king stages the farce of demon's surrender
black lives matter. white snow scatters

新奧爾良夏季的深紅色
橘黃色和淺黑色

野花抬起群山。夢遊
大地上升時，我飛在海上

女人的後裔，傷你的頭
撒旦的後裔，彼此為仇

魔王上演降魔的喜劇
黑命貴。白雪飛

Lay Still

lay still. in the right eye
lay still. on the wind-ravaged tombstone
lay still. staunch the bleeding in the scorching heat

seethe. in the gaps
seethe. on the eve of a journey
seethe. that fallen moment

靜 臥

靜臥。在右眼裡
靜臥。在狂風吹倒的墓碑上
靜臥。在炎熱裡止血

翻騰。在空白處
翻騰。在啟程的前夜
翻騰。在下墜的那一刻

Let

let me raise my dreamscape high, fill it with tragedy and suffering
that people on earth will no longer die of persecution

let prisoners lay bare freedom
turn hell into a kitchen

let rays of humanity ward off on the forehead
prevent evil-doers from raising their fists

讓

讓我把夢境騰空，存放悲劇與苦難
換取世上不再有冤死之人

讓囚徒們裸露出自由
把地獄改成廚房

讓人性之光擋在前額
阻止惡棍揮起

Peking Man

peking man bent down and walked through petrified mountain
grotto. raising battle ax and skull
missing link. archeologists can't find its heirs

floating in the cranium of antiquity

redeemers return to their native home
fire-roasted stag, hyena and saber-tooth tiger
fragments of bone. buried in ash

who are you? walking upright on two legs
foraging wild fruit. inventing needles to make clothes of hide
arranging funerary sacrifices for companions

you can't make a rubber band. you only die once
while we die again and again

北京猿人

北京猿人弓腰走出龍骨山
洞。舉起石斧和頭蓋骨
斷代後。考古者找不到進化鏈

顱骨裡飄蕩著，遠古

救贖者回到桑梓
火炙烤的雄鹿，鬣狗與劍齒虎
骨渣。壓在灰燼層

你們是誰。以下肢直立行走
採食野果。發明骨針縫製獸皮
給同伴準備殉葬品

你們造不出一根橡皮筋。只死一次
我們卻死很多次

Miracle

funeral held in the dead of night, seed cast off by the milky way
justices egg not yet emerged from its shell, on the rock face
no bridge leading to eternal paradise

veiled suffering, leaving flute holes on vertebra
defeated dusk, fallen black musical note
wind blows off offerings for relatives

神 蹟

深夜舉行葬禮。銀河撒下種子
正義的蛋尚未破殼。在陡崖
沒有橋通往恒久的樂土

被遮掩的苦難，在脊椎留下笛孔
潰散的黃昏，落下黑色音符
風吹斷親人的祭品

Hiccup

daybreak propped up on open wounds, breathing into bones
 wind, raises up the victim

's name carved on the wall
head askew looking at its own name. from the outside in

children, of the same grandmother
night, spilt bedpan
prosperity walls of bleached bones, shedding their own tears
hiccup

night of exploding red dwarf star. white dwarf in a blind
dashed. hiccup

呃

黎明撐開傷口，往骨骼吹氣
風，抬起遇難者

的，名字刻在牆上
它歪頭看著自己的名字。裡外看

子孫，來自同一個祖母
夜，滑出夜壺
白骨壘起的繁榮，每一根骨頭都會流淚
呃

紅矮星崩裂之夜。白矮星在盲區
撞擊。呃

Recall 12 Poems
追憶十二首
2018

Amsterdam's Egg

from the summit, from the split seams of the blue serene,
throw down the masks and blue dye for love,

river's reflection ripples on round breasts,
left and right in symmetry, light and dark face off,

yamen stiff as death, drops of water erode stone,
the grand eunuch escaping life to continue life,

阿姆斯特丹的蛋

從頂端，從蒼穹的破綻處，
為愛拋下口罩和顏料，

河流的反光，以弧線拂動圓乳，
左右對稱，明暗相峙，

僵死的衙門，滴水穿石，
內監為續命逃命，

Looking Back at Youth...

sleep at the edge of time. good traced back to its origins
faint distant light above, shine
corolla. surprise attack of the night breeze

you are benevolence, pried from the meteorite

you are the prime force. love's gravitational force...
the mirror shatters, slaves clamber from the deep...
death in stages, some slip quietly away...
some lie in the same place...

追憶似水年華……

睡在時間邊。追溯善的起源
天外微弱的光，映照
花冠。夜風襲

你是慈悲，撬起隕石

你是原動力。愛的引力……
鏡子裂開，奴隸們爬出深坑……
分期死亡，有人滑出原樣……
有人躺在原地……

Get Up, Bid Farewell to the Stone Age

                                        sever
midday. the plaster cast's left wrist severed
hanging down. half of the lips remain
brittle times. man of steel waves
to wake the feudal subjects' mal-intent

how would he use dialect to vanquish the world? ask the earth
if he dies, would we be better off

how many did october destroy! loved ones exterminate each other
do you believe? the hospital's low perimeter walls
branch in illusion. singing
the patient sinks into desperation. clings to his lies and doesn't let go

get up, the dawn is blooming
we climb over crumbling walls to bid farewell to the stone age

起來，告別石器時代

　　　　　　　　斷開
正午。石膏雕像的右臂斷開
垂下。嘴掉了半邊
易碎的時代。梟雄揮手
試圖喚醒臣民的惡念

以方言征服世界如何？問蒼茫大地
他死了，我們過得更好

十月曾毀滅多少人！親人相互毀滅
你相信嗎？醫院的圍牆裡
樹枝在幻影中。唱歌
陷入絕境的瘋子。抱著謊言不放

起來，日出已遍地開花
跨過殘垣，告別石器時代

Letter

—in memory of 1977

the prisoner for locked up twenty years receives a sudden letter from home
inconsolable, sobbing against the tree

facing the emptiness. ache
ache that splits the heart and lungs

twenty years without death. time peeling your chest and belly alive

heaven's singular lonely soul, howling at the jailor
head honcho omits ominous rays

ah! how many were torn from us by death, pounded to mincemeat

信

——紀念 1977

被關押二十年的囚徒，忽然收到家信
抱頭痛哭，抱樹痛哭

面對空。痛
撕心裂肺的痛。痛不欲生

二十年求死不能。活剝了開膛的光陰

天空唯有孤魂，向著獄卒哀嚎
牢頭，露兇光

啊！多少生離死別，被剁成肉醬

Bucket

bucket painted red, lost in Yuan dynasty
when I searched for it, my own face rippled in water

it was then that I learned evil follows on some people
the good are drops of tears filling up a bucket

carried by the floodwaters to the other shore, rays of sun cutting through its cracks
engulfed by ocean currents, swept away by the sea

there is no need to be in awe of the early nightfall
rippling in the bucket

桶

一個漆成紅色的桶，遺忘在元代
我詭探它時，臉在水裡晃動

當我得知，邪惡永久伴隨人類
善良化作淚水，滴入桶中

它被洪水沖上岸，光線射穿其豁口
它被洋流挾裹，被海潮托起

你不必敬畏黃昏
它在桶裡晃動

Observing Emptiness

win big
wēng ma ne bā mī mōu. buddha mounts a girl and ascends to heaven
wooden fish and lotus. buddha's desiccated head offered to
a museum. incantation clinches her

push the window open, droves of dawn's fish sleep in the sky
remains of man and animal, burning on the riverside
tree leaves fly, ash pounds life bare

空 觀

大樂透
嗡嘛呢叭咪吽。佛騎上少女升天
木魚蓮花。被割下的佛頭供於
博物館。咒語釘牢她

推開窗，黎明的魚群睡在天空
人和動物的殘骸，在恆河兩岸燃燒
樹葉飛起來，灰燼搗入生命

Void

yangtze river empty and unrestrained
orphaned crane chases the moon a thousand miles. tonight still

misses the ragged alms bowl of prehistory
you have what you wanted, the most beautiful
loved

you persevere in hollowing out a heart
like the most meticulous craftsman
I return you to that moment

空

萬古長江空自在
千里孤鶴追月。今夜還

錯過乞丐面前那只破損的史前空碗
你得到了想要的，最美的
喜愛的

你鍥而不舍地鏤空一顆心
如非凡的匠人
我帶你回歸那一刻

Light Lingers At Purgatory's Gates

a comb with broken teeth, untangling the seasons...

early hours. the city roves the precipitous cliff
seizing the convict's ruthless functionary, thinks up
evidence. playing with the newly concocted...

all that's left more than fate. more than life
the dead victorious

startled boorish man hides in the eucalyptus forest
rays of sunset, rumbling earth engulfing
empty space

光徘徊於煉獄之門

斷齒的梳子，為四季梳頭⋯⋯

凌晨。都市遊動到危崖
抓捕逃犯的酷吏，構想著
罪證。他把玩著剛剛捏造的⋯⋯

現在只剩下比命。比壽命
後死者勝

驚懼的莽漢藏身於案樹林
霞光，**轟**鳴地席卷
空白處

Live in Seclusion

silk clothes the conspiring official. golden age incurable

childhood. raised palanquin carries the flower queen
isle in flames, red eyes in flight

we set aside parasols and hard candy for children unknown
may they not fight with giants

隱 居

絲綢包起奸臣。盛世病入膏肓

童年。轎子抬走花魁
島嶼燃燒，如紅眼飛行

我們把傘和硬糖留給陌生的孩子
勸他們不要和猛獸搏鬥

Outside of the Human

november, lion pounced on the high platform
leaped out of last night
black tides flow by. familiar faces now disappeared
dragon ascends to the sky

wait a moment
it ought to have a bright future
Hong Kong, covered by red cloth dropping from the sky
bring out countless
injuries

人之外

十一月，獅子撲向高台
他跳出最後一夜
黑色潮水漫過。熟悉的臉消失
龍升天

等等
本應前程似錦的
香港，被從天而降的紅布蒙住了
扯出數不清的
傷

Cruiseship Passes Through Midnight's Strait

seawater surges with lust. foam pushed forth like an inheritance
low altitude moisture, cells dance in flight
unbounded sea, without surplus

storm bellows orders at the waves. monsoon casts seeds ashore
six months later, flowers flourishing
white seaside villa, earthly paradise
announcing spring's arrival

the repatriated man looks to the distance, powerless in the face of heresy
heaven and earth emerge white

遊輪駛過午夜的海峽

海水湧動生殖的欲望。泡沫如遺產推向遠處
低空的濕氣，細胞飛舞
無極的海面。沒有多余的

風暴怒吼驅趕著海浪。季風把種子拋入彼岸
六個月後，這裡花草繁茂
一棟白色的海邊別墅，世外桃源
宣告萬象更新

被遣返的老頭眺望著，他無力反駁邪說
天地呈現出白色

Desperate Straits

time erects a thousand-mile wall, the homeland under
heavy
                                        brick. watching over your
childhood. villages and paths have been caught up
the moon high, mountain collapses into the lake
married off. bloomed and departed

now, who's at the seaside weeping
autumn fallen ill, the war ends in winter
pterosaurs fly over the atlantic to breed their last
I am muddled mute. listening to the wind's slalom

絕 境

時間豎起萬里城牆，山河在
厚重的
　　　　　　　　磚下。看守你的
童年。捲起村莊與道路
月兒高，一座山坍塌在湖面
她嫁了。花開即永別

此刻，誰在海邊哭泣
秋天病了，戰爭在冬季結束
鳥掌龍飛越大西洋，為了最後一次繁殖
我暗啞了。聆聽風聲回旋

新人間351

右奈短詩選

作者	右 奈
插圖畫家	Clytze
英文編輯	Qu JingHua
特約校對	Jacqueline
主編	謝翠鈺
美術編輯	燕 妮

董事長	趙政岷
出版者	時報文化出版企業股份有限公司
	108019 台北市和平西路三段二四〇號七樓
	發行專線	(〇二) 二三〇六六八四二
	讀者服務專線	〇八〇〇二三一七〇五	(〇二) 二三〇四七一〇三
	讀者服務傳真	(〇二) 二三〇四六八五八
	郵撥	一九三四四七二四時報文化出版公司
	郵箱	一〇八九九 台北華江橋郵局第九九信箱
時報悅讀網	http://www.readingtimes.com.tw
法律顧問	理律法律事務所	陳長文律師、李念祖律師
印刷	國際彩印有限公司
初版一刷	二〇二二年四月八日
定價	新台幣四八〇元

(缺頁或破損的書,請寄回更換)

右奈短詩選/右奈作. -- 初版. -- 臺北市 : 時報文化
出版企業股份有限公司, 2022.04
　　面 ;　公分. -- (新人間 ; 351)
ISBN 978-626-335-121-9(平裝)

851.487　　　　　　　　　　　111002514

ISBN 978-626-335-121-9
Printed in Taiwan

右奈，1965 年 8 月出生，居住於香港。自幼喜歡唐詩。

15 歲寫了第一首詩：山川邊的油菜花開了 / 你不見了

隨著閱歷的豐富與視野的開闊，他的詩作風格變得抽象，具有夢幻性、原創性和悲劇性。

他以冷靜突兀的形式，構建新詩的美學畫面。試圖穩定漢字作為象形文字的原意與確定性。

他的詩主題是：生命的尊嚴與價值。他反對被奴役的人繼續奴役他人。

他追求漢語的純潔性與穿透力。是當代最傑出的抽象派詩人。

Yau Noi, born in August 1965, living in Hong Kong. He loves Tang poetry since he was little.
Wrote his first poem at the age of 15: "The rapeseed by the mountainside blooms; You are gone".
With his rich experience and broad horizon, the style of his works has become
abstract, full of dreaminess, originality and tragedy.
He constructs the aesthetic picture of Modern Chinese poetry in a calm and abrupt form. Try to
stabilize the original intention and certainty of Chinese characters as pictographs.
The theme of his poem is about the dignity and value of life. He opposed the people who have
been enslaved, continue to enslave others.
He pursues the purity and penetration of Chinese language, is the most outstanding contemporary abstract poet.

本書翻譯：
凱特·科斯特洛，譯者、牛津大學在讀博士。居住於新奧爾良。
Kate Costello is a translator and doctoral candidate at Oxford University.
She resides in New Orleans.